Itty ♥ Bitty PRINCESS Kitty

13

The Sweet Shop

by Melody Mews   illustrated by Ellen Stubbings

LITTLE SIMON

New York London Toronto Sydney New Delhi

This book is a work of fiction. Any references to historical events, real people, or real places are used fictitiously. Other names, characters, places, and events are products of the author's imagination, and any resemblance to actual events or places or persons, living or dead, is entirely coincidental.

LITTLE SIMON

An imprint of Simon & Schuster Children's Publishing Division

1230 Avenue of the Americas, New York, New York 10020

First Little Simon paperback edition March 2024

Copyright © 2024 by Simon & Schuster, LLC. Also available in a Little Simon hardcover edition.

All rights reserved, including the right of reproduction in whole or in part in any form.

LITTLE SIMON is a registered trademark of Simon & Schuster, LLC, and associated colophon is a trademark of Simon & Schuster, LLC.

Simon & Schuster: Celebrating 100 Years of Publishing in 2024

For information about special discounts for bulk purchases, please contact Simon & Schuster Special Sales at 1-866-506-1949 or business@simonandschuster.com.

The Simon & Schuster Speakers Bureau can bring authors to your live event. For more information or to book an event contact the Simon & Schuster Speakers Bureau at 1-866-248-3049 or visit our website at www.simonspeakers.com.

Designed by Laura Roode

Manufactured in the United States of America 0224 LAK

2 4 6 8 10 9 7 5 3 1

Library of Congress Cataloging-in-Publication Data

Names: Mews, Melody, author. | Stubbings, Ellen, illustrator. Title: The sweet shop / by Melody Mews ; illustrated by Ellen Stubbings. Description: First Little Simon paperback edition. | New York: Little Simon, 2024. | Series: Itty Bitty Princess Kitty; book 13 | Summary: "In the thirteenth Itty Bitty Princess Kitty chapter book, a new sweet shop comes to town and Lollyland is in for a real treat!"— Provided by publisher. Identifiers: LCCN 2023025169 (print) | LCCN 2023025170 (ebook) | ISBN 9781665953276 (paperback) | ISBN 9781665953283 (hardcover) | ISBN 9781665953290 (ebook) Subjects: CYAC: Cats—Fiction. | Princesses—Fiction. | Desserts—Fiction. | LCGFT: Novels. Classification: LCC PZ7.1.M4976 Sw 2024 (print) | LCC PZ7.1.M4976 (ebook) | DDC [Fic]—dc23

LC record available at https://lccn.loc.gov/2023025169

LC ebook record available at https://lccn.loc.gov/2023025170

Contents

Bunny's Best Books

"I love visiting your parents' bookstore," Itty Bitty Princess Kitty said to Chipper Bunny. Itty and Chipper were inside Chipper's family's bookshop, Bunny's Best Books. "There are *so* many books! And so many shoppers!"

"Everyone in Lollyland buys their books here," Chipper said proudly. "Maybe you'd like to buy one?"

"I'm sure the Princess already has a room full of books to read at the palace!" Chipper's mom, Mrs. Bunny, said.

"Actually," Itty said, "my dad's birthday is coming up. His favorite books are cookbooks."

"The King cooks?" Mrs. Bunny looked surprised.

Itty shook her head. "No. He likes to look at the pictures."

Chipper and his mom giggled.

"I'm not kidding," Itty replied. "He takes food *very* seriously."

The King of Lollyland did love to eat. Especially sweets. So much so that the kitchen fairies had banned him from the royal kitchen for sneaking too many treats.

Just then, the bell on the front door tinkled.

"Another customer!" Chipper cheered.

Itty glanced at the door and saw a shower of glitter that could mean only one thing: Luna Unicorn had arrived! Luna's horn spouted glitter whenever she was excited, which was often.

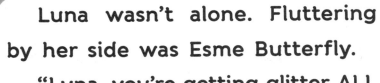

Luna wasn't alone. Fluttering by her side was Esme Butterfly.

"Luna, you're getting glitter ALL over the books!" Chipper grumbled.

"Oopsie," Luna said. "I'm sorry! I'll help clean it up!"

"Don't worry," Mrs. Bunny said kindly. "A little glitter only makes the books even more special. But do tell us what has you so excited."

Luna squeezed her eyes shut. Itty knew that look. Luna was trying to stop another glitter explosion.

"Why don't I tell everyone?" Esme asked. Luna nodded.

"A new shop is opening up across the street!" Esme announced. "And you'll never guess what it is!"

Pansy Panda

"A magic shop?" Itty guessed.

Esme shook her head.

"A musical instrument shop?"

"Nope," Esme said.

"We might be guessing all day," Chipper said. "Let's go see for ourselves!"

The friends rushed outside. They looked both ways to make sure no clouds were coming, then crossed the street.

"It's a sweet shop!" Chipper shouted.

Itty pushed her face up against the window, trying to look inside. Then someone opened the door.

"Hi!" Pansy Panda said. She went to the same school as Itty, Luna, Esme, and Chipper. "This is my dad's new shop! We're not open yet, but would you like a sample?"

"Sure!" Luna exclaimed.

Pansy led the way into the shop. There were still paint cans and boxes on the floor.

"It smells like maple syrup in here," Itty said.

"Good nose!" Pansy nodded. "Try a maple cream puff!"

Everyone helped themselves to a treat.

"These are soooo good," Esme said.

"Really soft and creamy!" Itty agreed.

"Is the syrup from Goodie Grove?" Chipper asked as he wiped his whiskers. Goodie Grove was the place in Lollyland where everyone went to get goodies.

There were cotton-candy bushes, a syrup river, and trees that grew lollipops and gumdrops.

"My dad gets all his ingredients from Goodie Grove, ever since he was just baking at home for fun," Pansy said. "But we haven't been able to visit recently. There's so much to do before opening day. I'm even missing school tomorrow to help my dad!"

"I can get some maple syrup for you tomorrow," Itty offered. "I'm going to Goodie Grove anyway. I go almost every day."

"*Everyone* does!" Luna added. "It's the *best* place to get treats in Lollyland. . . . Well, *one* of the best places," she said quickly. "I'm sure your dad's shop will be just as popular! And we'll help spread the word!"

Pansy thanked everyone.

"I'll see you tomorrow," Itty promised.

As she hopped onto a **cloud** back to the palace, Itty thought about how wonderful it was that the residents of Lollyland would soon have another place to go for treats. After all, if some treats were good, *more* treats were better!

The King's Lesson

"Guess what the new shop in Lollyland is going to be!"

It was dinnertime at the palace, but Itty was already thinking about desserts.

"A sweet shop," Itty's mom said between bites.

"Wait! How did you know?" Itty demanded.

"Darling, I am the Queen of Lollyland. I approve the new business permits."

Sometimes Itty forgot that her parents were the King and Queen. To her, they were just Mom and Dad.

"I wonder how the shop will do," the Queen continued. "Between Goodie Grove and the cooking fairies, Lollyland already has plenty of sweets."

"But Pansy's sweets are sooo yummy!" Itty declared.

"Yummier than Garbanzo's?" the King asked.

Garbanzo was the head chef in the royal kitchen. She was also the fairy who had banned the King from the kitchen. He had gone in one too many times to "taste test."

"Hmmm. Equally as good!" Itty replied.

"Speaking of sweets . . ." The King rose from his chair. He froze when Itty's mom gave him a stern look.

"You're not going into the kitchen, are you?" the Queen asked.

"Um . . ." The King sat down. "I was going to see if Garbanzo needed help with dessert."

"When was the last time the fairies allowed you to help in the kitchen?" the Queen asked pointedly.

"Never," the King mumbled.

It was true. The cooking fairies took care of all the cooking and baking, and they never allowed *anyone* to help.

Itty heard a thumping sound and looked down to see Garbanzo standing on the table, stomping her tiny feet.

"What's this about someone else's treats?" Garbanzo squeaked. "What kind of treat was it?"

Itty gulped. She hadn't realized Garbanzo was listening. "A maple cream puff," Itty said quietly.

"Hmph!" Garbanzo sniffed and flew away.

"I'd better go make sure she's okay," the King said as he rushed toward the kitchen.

"Your father will never learn," the Queen said, shaking her head.

chapter 4

Start Spreading the News

"There's a sweet shop opening downtown!" Itty told Tessa Tiger and Polly Porcupine. It was recess time. Instead of playing on the rainbow slide, Itty and Luna were spreading the word about Pansy's dad's shop.

Polly shrugged. "We get sweets from Goodie Grove."

"I'd rather go to Bunny's Best Books," Tessa added.

"Oh." Itty frowned. "Next time you're at Bunny's Best Books, check out the Sweet Shop too!"

"Why aren't they excited?" Luna wondered.

"Maybe they're not hungry," Itty replied. "Let's try again at Goodie Grove. Everyone there should be in the mood to think about treats!"

After school Itty and Luna hopped off a cloud as it pulled up to Goodie Grove. Chipper and Esme were already there.

"I'll get the maple syrup while you tell everyone about Pansy's shop," Itty said.

"I can come with you!" Chipper offered.

Itty thought about the times Chipper had gotten chased off by the syrup fairies for not following their rules. She shook her head.

Itty waited patiently as the fairies gathered buckets of syrup for her.

"Is Garbanzo making a special cake for the King?" a fairy named Nougat asked.

"It's for my friend Pansy," Itty explained. "Her dad is opening a sweet shop downtown."

Nougat rested on Itty's shoulder. "Is he a fairy?"

"Nope, but his treats are delicious!" Itty promised. "You should try them!"

Itty was pretty sure she saw the tiny fairy frown before she flew away.

Itty's friends joined her to help carry the buckets to the Sweet Shop. "Were the animals excited to hear about the shop?" Itty asked.

"I'm not sure," Esme admitted.
"But I told everyone!"

"Me too," Luna added.

"Me three." Chipper
nodded. "Now I have
a very important
question. . . . Are
we going to have
a snack here at Goodie
Grove, or wait until we get to the
Sweet Shop?"

Itty giggled
and said, "Why
not both?"

Grand Opening Eve

"It looks beautiful in here!" Itty said as they entered the Sweet Shop. The walls were painted with swirling rainbow ribbons, and the floor looked like it was paved with gumdrops.

"It smells even better!" Chipper said as he rubbed his tummy.

Sparkling glass cases were filled with delicious-looking tarts, cookies, pies, and cupcakes.

Gleaming silver trays held the shop's special maple puffs and a few other goodies that Itty couldn't wait to sample.

Pansy smiled proudly. Her dad came out of the back kitchen. "Is there anything else I need before the grand opening tomorrow?" he asked.

Itty looked around. It did look wonderful . . . but was *something* missing?

"I know!" Itty said. "You need a menu!"

"That's a great idea!" Mr. Panda said. "Pansy, my paws are covered in dough. Would you make a sign that lists everything we're selling?"

Pansy bit her lip. "I don't have nice paw-writing. It might not look very nice if I make it."

"That's what friends are for!" Luna assured her.

Chipper gathered art supplies for the sign. Itty used her best paw-writing to neatly list all the treats that would be for sale, and

Esme decorated the sign with colorful drawings of flowers. Then Luna added the finishing touch: glitter!

"*Now* the shop is ready for the grand opening!" Pansy declared as she hung the sign on the wall. "I can't wait for tomorrow!"

"Neither can we," Itty cheered. "I should warn you, though. My dad has a sweet tooth, so you might want to tell him there's a limit to the free samples he can have!"

"Your dad is coming tomorrow?" Pansy looked surprised.

"Of course! And my mom, too!"

Pansy gulped. Now she looked surprised *and* nervous. "The King and Queen of Lollyland will be at *our* shop?"

"They'll love your dad's treats!" Itty said. "I just know your grand opening is going to be a sweet success!"

The Not-So-Big Day

The next morning, Itty and her parents arrived at the Sweet Shop just as the mermaids from Mermaid Cove were singing the time. Itty heard eleven notes. It was eleven o'clock—time for the grand opening of the Sweet Shop!

"Thank you so much for coming!" Pansy exclaimed as she ushered them inside. The shop looked extra special with twinkling lights strung around the display cases.

"Your shop is lovely," the Queen said.

"It smells incredible," the King added. "May I?" He gestured toward a table filled with samples. Itty spotted maple puffs, marshmallow cookies, raspberry doughnuts, and cupcakes with swirling frosting.

"Please help yourself," Mr. Panda said.

"Try the maple puffs," Itty chimed in.

"Make sure to leave some for the rest of the kingdom," the Queen added.

"Are we the first to arrive?"
Itty asked as she glanced around
the otherwise empty shop. Pansy
nodded.

"Don't worry. People will start showing up soon!" Itty said, trying to cheer up her worried friend.

And people did show up: Luna, Esme, and Chipper, to be exact. But even after the mermaids sang twelve notes, no one else came.

All the yummy-looking treats sat uneaten in their cases. Pansy went from looking worried to looking very sad. Itty felt terrible. Where was everyone?

The King bought another treat (his sixth, by Itty's count). He smiled kindly at Pansy. "Your father's sweets are truly delicious," he boomed. "And I am an **expert** in the sweets department!"

Pansy smiled a wobbly smile.

"Shall I issue a royal decree?" the King suggested. "I can tell all of Lollyland to try out your shop."

Mr. Panda shook his head. "Thank you, King Kitty, but I don't want animals to feel like they *have* to come. I want them to come because they *want* to."

Itty understood what Mr. Panda meant. Even so, she couldn't help but wonder: How could they get the creatures of Lollyland to *want* to come?

Fairy Good Advice

That evening Itty was curled up in a squishy chair filled with magic beans, staring at her glowing shooting star in its case. It was Itty's eighth shooting star, the one that had made her the Princess of Lollyland.

Itty heard tapping at her window. Her fairy friend Bree was outside!

"Why do you look sad?" Bree asked as she fluttered into the room.

"No one came to the grand opening of the Sweet Shop today," Itty explained. "My friend Pansy was disappointed, and I feel bad."

"Are the sweets yummy?" Bree asked.

"They're sooo yummy!" Itty exclaimed. "My dad likes them so much that he brought home leftovers. My mom told him Garbanzo won't appreciate having treats in the palace that someone else made, but he insisted."

Bree giggled. She knew about the King's sweet tooth and how fussy Garbanzo could be.

In fact, Bree was probably the only laid-back fairy in all of Lollyland. Most fairies took their jobs very seriously and insisted on doing things their way.

It had been hard for Bree to fit in with the other fairies in Lollyland at first.

"Some things take time," Bree said. "Remember what a tough time I had figuring out where I belong?"

Itty nodded. "Yes, but look at you now! You're one of the best builder fairies in all of Lollyland, and you have so many fairy friends!"

Bree smiled proudly. "Thank you! But that's because you didn't give up on me. Your friend Pansy and her dad just need time. And maybe some help from their good friend Princess Itty."

The worried feeling in Itty's tummy eased up.

Bree was right. All Itty needed was a plan.

Itty's tummy rumbled, and she realized that maybe she *also* needed a snack.

Hopefully the King hadn't eaten all the leftovers!

chapter 8

Itty Has
an Idea

The next day, Itty sent a messenger fairy to Luna, Esme, and Chipper asking them to meet downtown. Her plan was to walk around and ask the residents of Lollyland why they had not come to the grand opening.

After the friends met up, Itty noticed someone waving from across the street. It was Pansy!

"Hi, Pansy!" Luna said. "Are you on your way to the shop?"

"Actually, I just left the shop," Pansy said. "My dad didn't need me to help out because . . ." Itty didn't need her to finish the sentence to understand. The Sweet Shop still didn't have customers.

Luna told Pansy about their plan. Pansy wanted to join too. "I would do anything to help my dad's shop," she said.

Itty, Pansy, and Chipper took the north side of Main Street. Esme and Luna took the south side.

First Itty, Pansy, and Chipper asked a mother bear pushing a stroller. "Yesterday was busy for me," the mother said. "I had to take my twins for a fur cut. Besides, we can get our treats from Goodie Grove."

"My cooking fairies make sure we have plenty of delicious treats at home," a panther told them. "I don't want to hurt their feelings."

Everyone had similar answers. They had been too busy to go to the grand opening, or they felt like they didn't *need* to go because they already had Goodie Grove and the cooking fairies.

Itty and her friends walked over to the Sweet Shop. Pansy's dad was happy to see them, but no other customers were in sight.

"I don't understand. I would walk all the way across town to eat this maple puff," Luna said between bites.

Then the door to the shop opened, and Garbanzo fluttered inside!

"Is this the shop that sells the maple puffs?" Garbanzo asked. She was not smiling.

Oh no, Itty thought. *Is she mad because Dad brought the leftovers back to the palace?*

"Yes. Welcome to the Sweet Shop!" Mr. Panda replied.

"I'll take ten, please," Garbanzo said, opening her change purse and putting a few coins on the countertop.

Itty stared in shock. Garbanzo was buying someone else's food?

"What?" Garbanzo demanded as Itty continued to stare. "I tried one of the puffs your dad brought home. They *are* delicious!"

Pansy handed the box of puffs over to Garbanzo. "Thank you so much, but . . . can't you just make your own?"

"It's nice to enjoy something someone else made for once," Garbanzo huffed. "We fairies don't mind eating treats that others have made, as long as they meet our standards. And these"— Garbanzo shook the box—"are definitely delicious."

"Please tell your friends!" Pansy said as Garbanzo flew away.

"If the pickiest food fairy loves your treats, all of Lollyland will!" Chipper said to Mr. Panda. "Now we just need Garbanzo to spread the word."

A bright smile lit up Itty's face. "I just thought of a way we can spread the word too!" she said.

A Food Cloud

"A food cloud?" Pansy repeated.

"It would be like a traveling, pop-up Sweet Shop!" Itty explained. "We can park a cloud at Goodie Grove and sell sweets. We would give out a lot of samples, too!"

"What a great idea!" Esme said. "Once everyone gets a taste, they'll know that it's worth visiting the shop!"

At first Mr. Panda seemed hesitant. "Garbanzo liked my sweets, but what if the fairies at Goodie Grove get upset? What if they don't like my sweets?"

"You already got a seal of approval from the King, the Queen, and the head of the royal kitchen," Itty said. Then she did a little curtsy. "*And the Princess of Lollyland, of course!*"

"And your daughter, who thinks your sweets are the best in the world!" Pansy added.

Mr. Panda smiled and gave his daughter a hug. "Thank you, girls," he said. "Now, how exactly would this food cloud work?"

That weekend Mr. Panda set up a food cloud in front of Goodie Grove. Thanks to the glittery signs that Luna had created, no one could miss it.

THE SWEET SHOP

Itty and her friends helped at the food cloud too. They all wore matching aprons that Coco, the royal seamstress, had made for them. "The Sweet Shop" was stitched in rainbow thread on the front. Itty wore her blouse with puffy sleeves under the apron. The sleeves reminded her of the maple cream puffs!

The Sweet Shop food cloud was a success. The first day, the food cloud ran out of samples before lunchtime. The next day, Pansy's dad baked double batches and still ran out of treats.

Lollyland loved Pansy's dad's sweets. And his number one fans were the fairies! The Goodie Grove fairies were proud that someone was using their ingredients to make something so delicious.

All the cooking fairies went to Goodie Grove, and they weren't picking up ingredients for their own cooking. They were treating themselves to dessert that someone else had prepared.

The panther that Itty had talked to on Main Street visited too. "I can't believe my cooking fairy recommended food made by someone else," he said. "But now I understand why!"

Pansy also gave out a flyer to every customer. "Please come to the grand reopening tomorrow," she said.

"We'll be there," the customers promised.

The Grand Reopening

The next afternoon, Itty and her parents arrived at the Sweet Shop just as they had the week before. This time there was a line of customers around the block!

Everyone stepped aside for the King and Queen of Lollyland.

But the Queen waved everyone inside ahead of them. Itty and her parents went to the back of the line to wait patiently. Well, the King was not very good at being patient, but he tried his best.

Soon they were inside. After Itty got her paws on a strawberry pie, Esme, Luna, and Chipper appeared.

"The grand reopening is a grand success!" Luna exclaimed in a cloud of glitter.

Pansy popped up by Luna's side. "It's all thanks to the four of you.

Thank you for helping and not giving up on the shop. This is my dad's and my dream come true!"

"That's what friends are for," Itty said.

THE SWEET SHOP

Just as the last customer in line left the store, Mr. Panda came over. "Good news!" he said. "I have to close up shop for the day."

"How is that good news?" Esme asked.

Mr. Panda gestured to the glass cases. "It's because we've sold out of everything!" he said proudly. Everyone clapped in excitement, and Pansy gave her dad a hug to congratulate him.

"Does that mean I can't buy more to take home?" King Kitty said, sadly rubbing his tummy. Queen Kitty tried to scold him, but Mr. Panda pulled out a box from under the counter.

Inside the box were mini cupcakes frosted to look just like the King, the Queen, and the Princess. Itty gasped in delight. "I've never seen anything like it!" she said.

Pansy linked her arm through Itty's and smiled. She said, "The Sweet Shop is lucky to have such loyal and royal customers. Come again soon!"

Heart Candy Cake

Maple Cream Puffs

Starry Cupcakes

Apple Pie

Cherry Pie

Mini Carrot Cakes

Chiffon Cake

Chocolate Chip Cookies

Strawberry Shortcake

Marshmallow Pies

Cranberry Muffins

Red Velvet Cake

Itty has lots of stories to share!

If you like Itty's adventures,
then you'll love . . .